What Am I Fe

Defining Emotions

By Katie Flanagan

Illustrated by Anna Krupa

Grosvenor House
Publishing Limited

MW00892691

The right of Katie Flanagan to be identified as the author of this
work has been asserted in accordance with Section 78
of the Copyright, Designs and Patents Act 1988

The book cover picture is copyright to Katie Flanagan

This book is published by
Grosvenor House Publishing Ltd
Link House
140 The Broadway, Tolworth, Surrey, KT6 7HT.
www.grosvenorhousepublishing.co.uk

A CIP record for this book
is available from the British Library

ISBN 978-1-78623-991-4

Dedications:

For Maisie and Robbie

Please visit https;//www.NEG4Kids.co.uk for more information, ideas, examples and new books.

If you like this book you may also like:

What am I feeling? My feelings journal.

Soon to be released:

What Else am I feeling?

What Else am I feeling? My feelings journal.

Emotional Literacy

Foreword For Adults

Emotional literacy is the ability to be able to know, understand, voice and process our feelings. The better we are at developing our self-awareness in this way, the more positive relationships we can have with ourselves and those around us.

Helping children develop their emotional literacy skills is one of the most important things we can do as parents, carers and educators. It can have a lifelong fundamentally positive impact on their self-esteem, mental health, independence, behaviour and resilience in managing life's challenges and experiences. The more accurately we can teach children to know and describe their feelings the more we can help them to learn to meet their needs when they experience those emotions, therefore allowing the feelings to pass more easily.

The more time we spend with children, supporting them with developing these skills the better. Emotional Literacy is a relatively new concept in the field of education and parenting. It can be very challenging even for some of us as adults if we haven't had the opportunities to develop our own emotional literacy skills. Hopefully this book will support you in opening up these useful discussions with the children you care for or teach. You can support your child in their journey and even learn and grow together sharing your emotional experiences and thinking about ways to process these emotions in a positive, healthy way.

How to make the most of this book!

Talking about the content

This book aims to help promote discussion between adults and children about feelings. Some of the scenarios may not represent how your child feels and they may experience other emotions too. This can be a really good start for discussion and self-awareness to help them challenge their own thoughts about their feelings and when they experience them and to understand that it is not always the same for everyone.

Here are some examples of questions you can use to prompt discussion, to both ask the child and/or provide modelling to support them in recognising facial expressions, feelings and experiences of feelings. You can use a mirror to help you look at facial expressions.

Recognising emotions in ourselves

- **Facial expressions and behaviour**

  Can you make your face look like you're feeling...?

  Can you show me your... face? Do you think my face looks...? How do you know? What are my eyebrows doing?

  What is my/your mouth doing?

  Have you ever felt...? I sometimes feel...?

When did you last feel...? The last time I felt... was when...

Where do you feel it in your body when you feel...? When I feel... I feel it...? (E.g. when I feel angry I feel it in my head, when I feel worried I get butterflies in my tummy.)

If you don't know maybe think about it or notice what happens when you feel... for next time we read the book.

- **Experiences**

What do you do when you feel...? (E.g. I sometimes don't talk when I feel shy, or I jump around when I'm excited, I shout when I'm angry, I look down when I'm embarrassed.)

What sort of things do you think might make you feel...? I feel... when ...

Have you ever seen anyone who might have been feeling...? What did they do? I saw ... when they were feeling... and I noticed they...?

Do the feelings always feel the same strength or does it change? Do they feel less powerful at times?

- **Discussion about having more than one feeling in a situation**

What other feelings do you think they might have here?

Do you think they are just feeling angry or could they be feeling sad as well?

Have you ever felt two emotions or even more at the same time? Happy and sad at the same time or excited and proud?

What happens if you don't tell anyone about your feelings? Does it go away more quickly, slowly, or does it lead to more tricky feelings like anger or sadness?

Recognising emotions in others

What do you notice about the characters facial expression when they're feeling...?

What does their body language look like?

Why do you think the character is feeling e.g. angry, sad?

I think I would feel... and... if that happened to me

- **Taking responsibility for ourselves when responding to others feelings?**

What can you do if someone is showing... feelings and behaviour?

What can you do if you see someone feeling...? (E.g. if someone is being angry you can walk away).

It's not our job to fix other people's feelings and we don't have to stay around if someone's behaviour is hurtful or unsafe. But if we want to choose to help them can you think of some kind ways you can help (if we are happy to do that and, if it's safe for us to do so)?

You can use the 'What am I feeling?' activity journal available to write down your ideas and draw pictures of your face and what you do when you've got these different feelings. There is also more guidance and ideas for developing strategies in the journal.

HOW TO MAKE THE MOST OF THIS BOOK!

Talking about different words for the same feelings

Sometimes, but not always, feelings can also have different words.
You may think the words are grown up for children but you'll be surprised how much they can learn
and how empowered they feel using the right words for the right feelings.

Angry – cross, rageful, furious, annoyed
Happy – elated, joyful, delighted
Anxious – fearful, worried, scared, nervous
Embarrassed – ashamed, self-conscious
Tired – sleepy, exhausted, lethargic
Relaxed – calm, serene, tranquil
Sad – down, low, upset
Disappointed – discontent, let down, disenchanted, discouraged
Shy – cautious, timid, coy, wary, nervous
Bored – disinterested, dull
Safe – protected, secure
Proud – contented, honoured
Surprised – shocked, amazed, startled
Excited – overjoyed, thrilled, enthusiastic
Jealous – envious, possessive

You can ask your child:

Can you think of any more words yourself?
You could use the feelings journal available to write down your ideas
of the different words or favourite word you use for your feelings.

How to make the most of this book!

Talking about different strategies to help us process these feelings

One of the most important things to help children cope with their feelings, especially the more unpleasant ones, is to help them learn and think about strategies they can use, when they have those feelings, to make them feel better. This can help children to become more independent in managing their feelings and behaviour. The more they can talk about their emotions and find ways to manage them independently by putting strategies into practice, the more it will help them as they grow older and experience more challenging situations in their lives. The greater ownership children can take in developing their own strategies, the more effective it will be for them. There are some ideas listed below, but feel free to support your child in thinking of, and practicing, strategies that are right for them. It's also really important for us as adults to model as best we can and to appreciate how hard it is for us to change our behaviour, and so it is equally challenging for children. Being as patient and understanding with them, and ourselves, as possible will really help when trying to implement new strategies especially for the more difficult feelings.

The most effective thing is for children to find the best strategies that are right for them.

Developing the right strategies for your child isn't always easy and simple, but here are some ideas of strategies you could try:

Firstly, if possible, it's always good to help the child say I feel... naming the feeling is essential to understanding it and taking ownership of how they feel.

Help your child remember that all feelings pass and the more we can talk about them and find something positive to do the quicker they will pass. You can help them to try and scale them on a scale of 0 – 10 and to help them realise that feelings aren't always experienced at the same level of intensity and it can change and eventually become a 0!

You could talk about what would help make small steps to get to an 8 or a 7.

When talking to your children about their feelings using less directed talk can be really helpful:

You look like you're feeling... You sound like you're feeling... I want to listen to what you're trying to tell me, but I can't hear what you are saying through your....crying, shouting, silence.

You can front what you say to your child with something positive about the child first so, 'You are such a calm and kind little girl/boy so tell me about why you felt so angry that you hit your friend'.

Another way of being positive with your child is by saying you're such a kind/gentle boy/girl that this hitting behaviour doesn't match what I know about you, so why don't we unpick how you're feeling to work out what is going on for you and see if we can help you be the kind boy/girl that we both know you are.

Modelling strategies as a parent are also extremely powerful for children even if you have to 'pretend' or role play at first.

You can find more specific ideas and strategies for each emotion in the 'What am I feeling' Journal book.

WHAT ARE FEELINGS?

A foreword for children

Feelings are the way our body reacts to our thoughts and the things that happen around us. Our brain is like a computer and helps us makes sense of things that happen to us and around us. This can then create feelings and often feelings can affect the way we behave too.

We all get lots of different feelings throughout our day. Some feelings are enjoyable and others can be less enjoyable. Sometimes our feelings just pass through us as they are meant to, but other times they get stuck and we need to do something to help them pass through in the most positive way possible. The best way to help them pass is to **feel** them, **talk** about them and then **do** something to help them pass. But in order to talk about them we need to know what they are and times when we might experience them.

This book can help you to define and know what your feelings are and support you in exploring and thinking about times when you might experience them. Not everyone gets the same feelings in the same situations, so you might like to think of your own example of when you get that feeling too. You can talk with your grown up about when they get feelings too and think about ways to help them get easier and pass.

Some of these feelings you might already know the words for and others might be new to you. Some feelings have lots of different words that help describe them as well, see if you can think of some. Now you know the names for some feelings you can use these when you're reading other story books and see if you can work out how the characters might be feeling too!

When good things happen or I'm doing something I enjoy

I feel happy ...

...like when I'm having fun and
playing with my friends.

When something happens that I don't want to happen want to happen

I feel angry ...

...like when my favourite toy gets broken.

If something upsets me

I feel sad...

...like when I lost my favourite toy.

When I haven't had much sleep, or
I've had a busy day and need a rest

I feel tired...

...like when I have had a late night
or when I've been running around
in the park all day!

When I know I'm being looked after

I feel safe...

...like when a grown up holds my
hand when we're crossing the road.

If I think something bad might happen

I feel anxious...

... like when I see people arguing and I don't know what will happen next.

Sometimes when I don't know people or situations very well

I feel shy...

...like when I meet someone new for the first time.

When I know something really fun
is going to happen

I feel excited...

...like when I'm opening my presents on Christmas day!

If I haven't got anything interesting
or fun to do

I feel bored...

...like when I'm going on a long car journey with nothing to do!

If something really exciting doesn't happen

I feel disappointed...

...like when I couldn't go to my friend's birthday party because I was poorly.

When something happens that I wasn't expecting

I feel surprised...

...like when it started snowing!

Sometimes when someone has something or someone's attention that I would like too

I feel jealous...

...like when I'm watching someone else opening their birthday presents and I wish it was my birthday too!

Sometimes if I make a mistake, do something silly, or when people are looking at me and I don't want them to

I feel embarrassed...

...like when I was trying to answer a question in class and people were laughing at me.

If I've done something really well and tried my best

I feel proud...

...like when I show someone special
the best picture I've done.

When my body is still and I'm not
thinking about things too much

I feel relaxed...

...like when I'm cuddling up at bedtime listening to a story!

All these feelings,
Well, they're ok,
I get lots of different feelings,
Throughout my day,
Knowing what they are
and knowing what to say
will help me feel happier in every way,
When things are tricky, I'll know what to do
Because I have shared this book with you
It will help me have a better day
In my learning and my play!

CPSIA information can be obtained
at www.ICGtesting.com
Printed in the USA
BVHW021507120320
574849BV00005B/182

9 781786 239914